The Space Hut

WEEKLY READER
CHILDREN'S BOOK CLUB

Weekly Reader
Children's Book Club
presents

The Space Hut

Illustrated by Leo Summers

By Ester Wier

STACKPOLE BOOKS

Harrisburg, Pennsylvania

THE SPACE HUT

Published by
STACKPOLE BOOKS
Cameron and Kelker Streets
Harrisburg, Pa. 17105

Library of Congress Catalog Card Number 67-21673
Printed in U.S.A.

Weekly Reader Book Club Edition
Intermediate Division

The Space Hut

Chapter 1

*S*omething happened to Mike McAllister the first time he climbed to the top of the oak tree.

It was in December, on the day they moved into the new house in the new town, and the snow lay on the ground and the wind whipped icily up and down the street. He went directly to have a look at the back yard when they arrived at the house.

His father, who had bought the house the week before and who had met them that morning at the railroad station, hadn't said a word about the tree on the drive to their new home. He had told Mike about the basement with a special corner for the workbench and tools, about his plans for finishing the rest of it off as a recreation room, about the power lawn mower that had come with the place, about his school only three blocks away. Maybe his father hadn't noticed the tree although how anyone could overlook the gaunt skeleton-like giant standing at the corner of the yard, its bare branches flung out like great arms, Mike couldn't imagine.

He went up to it and laid his hands on the rough bark, gazing up, up, up to the very top. There was a special sound as the gusts rushed through its branches, like logs crackling in the fireplace on a cold night, like river ice breaking up in the spring, like old bones rattling together.

Then, almost before he knew it, he was shinnying up the trunk and climbing from branch to branch until he could go no farther. Below, the houses and yards of the neighborhood shrank in size and the streets became a mathematical arrangement of neat squares. Towering over everything in the area, he looked far across the countryside and saw a frozen river, glinting like a silver trail as it twisted down from the distant hills.

He had clung to the upper branches until his fingers grew numb and his ears felt like chunks of ice against his head; then slowly, carefully, he climbed back to the ground. For the rest of the day he had walked around as though only part of him had come down out of the tree.

Up there he had suddenly become aware of a different and wonderful feeling. It wasn't just height, because height wasn't anything new to him. Their apartment in the city had been on the eighth floor, so he was used

to it. This was different. It was as if all the ties of earth fell away and he was free as a bird, or an astronaut with space all around and beyond him. From now on he knew he had to be part of that world up there, a world without boundaries or limits, a world that could belong to anyone who had the daring and courage to seek it out and claim it.

When he finally went inside the house, his father beckoned to him and he went to where his parents stood at the top of the basement stairs. "We've gotten this far on our tour of the house, Mike," Mr. McAllister said. "Let's all go down to the basement together." His father put his hand on the door knob, then turned back to face him and his mother.

"There's something I haven't told you two about," he said, casting a worried glance at his wife. "Remember how the man we bought the house from did us a favor by moving out of it ahead of time so we could move right in? It meant you two could join me right away instead of waiting there in the city for another few weeks. He didn't have to do it and I appreciated it so when he asked me to do him a favor, I couldn't refuse, could I?"

Mike watched his father. It wasn't like him not to say right out what was bothering him. His mother was watching too, a curious look on her face.

"What was the favor?" she asked.

Mr. McAllister started to answer, then shrugged his shoulders instead. "Easier to show you than to tell you. Come on downstairs."

They followed him into the basement which was a

long empty room, with a bare cement floor and brick walls. In one corner there was a small cage.

His father pointed toward it. "It's a kind of . . . well, a . . . a pet. The man couldn't take it with him because he's going to a new job overseas so I promised him we'd take care of it, give it a home." His eyes were still fixed on his wife.

Mike ran across the room and peered through the wire mesh. Inside was a small animal about the size of a cat, its fur black with two white stripes running down its back. It lay curled in a ball in one corner of the cage.

"Good heavens!" his mother exclaimed when she saw it. "It's a skunk!"

The animal, hearing voices, raised its small head and looked at them, its long pointed muzzle quivering, its eyes bright and curious. Mrs. McAllister backed away hurriedly. "A skunk!" she repeated. "Don't frighten it, Mike. It's apt to . . . well, everyone knows what a skunk is apt to do when it's frightened. Come away, son." She turned to her husband. "That's a wild animal, George. It might . . . oh, dear . . ."

Mike's father laid a hand on her arm. "It can't do what you're thinking because it's been fixed . . . and it isn't wild, it's tame. The man said it was very gentle and a good pet and that it would keep our garden free of insects . . ."

Her son could see that although she still wasn't convinced, the part about the insects appealed to her. What she had missed most in the big city apartment had been her garden. "I'd hoped Mike could have a dog now that we're in a house of our own, but since you promised . . ." She looked worried. "What do you think of a skunk for a pet, son?"

Mike had never before seen a skunk alive and breathing and within arm's reach, so he knelt down to study the animal. Thrusting a finger through the wire mesh, he wiggled it. The skunk uncurled itself, raised a bushy plume of a tail, stretched it short legs, then came over to inspect Mike's finger. It winked one small bright eye, then yawned, showing a row of sharp white teeth.

"I like the idea fine," Mike said. "What's his name?"

Mr. McAllister looked surprised. "Why, I never thought to ask. We had so many other things to talk about."

"Then I'll have to name him, won't I? Can I choose any name I want?"

"Sure," said his father. "He's going to be your pet."

Mike had the name ready. "Beetlejuice. That's it. Beetlejuice."

His mother was puzzled. "What an odd name. Why would you want to call him that?"

"It's the name of a star," Mr. McAllister explained. "One of the stars used to navigate by. I've told Mike about it. I think he can even pick it out himself in the night sky. You spell it B-e-t-e-l-g-e-u-s-e, but it's pronounced the way he says it."

Mike didn't know exactly why he wanted to name the skunk for the star. Maybe it was so it too could have some part in the new and wonderful world he had only just discovered himself up there in the tree today.

"Can I pick him up?" he asked.

"Maybe he'll bite," his mother said, timidly.

"No, he won't," Mike assured her, "or he'd already have bitten my finger." Reaching into the cage he found that the skunk came to his hands, waiting to be lifted out. Mike held him carefully and the animal seemed content, snuggling down into the crook of the boy's arm. It stayed there for a few minutes, then climbed up Mike's arm, its long toes gripping his sleeve, and lay across his shoulders, holding on with its claws.

"That's the way the man carried him," Mr. McAllister said. "First time I came to see the house he answered the door with the skunk draped over his shoulders just like that. Gave me quite a surprise."

Chapter 2

The idea of building a hut up in the tree came to Mike the second time he climbed the tree, a week later. It was such an exciting idea that he slid most of the way down the trunk and ran into the house to find the phone book and look up the address of the nearest lumber yard. He went there after lunch, anxious to find out what wood for a hut would cost.

"What kind do you want?" the man in the office asked him.

Mike shrugged. "I don't know. Just wood I guess. How much is it?"

"Depends. We've got pine, mahogany, oak, almost any kind you can name. How much would you need?"

Mike didn't know.

"What's it for?"

Mike hesitated, then said, "A hut. A tree hut."

The man shook his head. "You don't want to buy wood here. It would run you twenty, thirty dollars maybe. When I was a kid, we used to use old boxes, old crates, anything we could get our hands on for free. You don't need expensive wood like I sell for a hut. Any old thing will do."

Mike felt pretty discouraged as he walked home. Any old thing wouldn't do for the kind of hut he wanted to build. But how was he ever to get the money he would need? Even if he saved his allowance and whatever he could make shoveling snow for the neighbors it wouldn't add up fast enough. His father had said that next year when he was twelve he could try for a paper route but he couldn't wait that long. He had to build the hut this spring! He had to have it this summer! He thought of asking his father to let him have money enough for lumber but, remembering that his mother had told him how little there would be for extras now after buying a new house and setting up a new law practice in a new town, he decided against it.

During the following week, he felt sad whenever he thought about the hut. Then, on Saturday, while he was sitting on the front steps with Beetlejuice clinging to his shoulders, he saw a delivery van draw up in front of the house next door. Whatever their neighbors, the Williamses, had bought required a mighty big truck to deliver it. Watching the four husky men haul and shove and lift the huge crate, it came to him that here was the wood he needed. With a leap he was off the porch and knocking at Mrs. Williams' front door.

"Can I have the wood in that crate they're delivering?" he asked when she came to answer.

Warily, keeping her eye on Beetlejuice, she said, "You can have anything you want, Mike, if you'll just take that animal away." Mike had noticed that most people grew nervous whenever they got close to a skunk. "As soon as the men get the crating off the freezer, I'll have them leave it in the yard."

"I'll shovel your snow for a month for nothing," Mike promised joyfully. "I need that wood bad. It's just what I've been looking all over for. I'll run your errands and clean your garage out too."

She held up a hand. "You can have it for nothing if you'll just take that . . . that creature away."

The crating was exactly right. It was smooth and strong, the planks just the right size and there was enough of it to make a good-sized hut. He was grateful that the Williamses had felt they needed an extra-large freezer. After removing the nails, he stacked it under the porch. Then he laid a tarpaulin he found in the garage over it, hoping to keep it from warping in the wet weather that still lay ahead.

Now he began to make his plans. He knew it had to be done carefully if he were to succeed in building the kind of hut he had in mind. He had the wood so the first

hurdle was passed. The next one would be getting per-mission to build the hut into the tree.

Every night he drew sketches, figuring out a place for each board. Most of his waking moments were spent dreaming about the hut. Setting aside the precious hour between finishing his homework for school and bedtime, he worked at his plans, neglecting his stamp collection, his model planes, TV, even Beetlejuice.

When the hut was finished, he would ask his new school friends over to see it. He would call it a space hut. Most of the boys he knew intended to be spacemen when they grew up and at the top of the tree they could pre-tend they were about to take off on an orbit around the earth or on a moon shot or on an exploratory trip to the planets. How much nearer their dreams would seem up there so close to the sky!

Finally his plans were finished. He had figured where each plank was to go, where every nail belonged. The weather began to grow milder and he knew that now was the time to tell his mother about the hut and get her permission to build it. If she agreed, she would talk to his father and then he could begin the actual building.

He found her out in the yard, turning the earth over, digging a bed for her flower garden. With Beetlejuice across his shoulders to give him moral support, he crossed the grass to stand beside her.

"Please," he started out, "just listen while I tell you what's on my mind. Don't say anything until I finish." He had the speech all rehearsed and a question from her at the wrong time could make him forget part of it.

She sat back on her heels and heard him out. When he was done, almost out of breath from talking so fast, he thought he saw a faint smile in her eyes. She laid down the trowel, then stood up, measuring herself against him.

"You're almost as tall as I am, Michael," she said, and he wondered what that had to do with building a tree hut. Turning, she looked at the huge oak for a long time.

"You're growing up and now you have the first real dream of your own. I'll worry about you scampering up and down such a big tree, I guess, but I can't stand in the way of that dream. Right now I'm sure I know just how an astronaut's mother must feel." She smiled. "I'll talk to your father."

Mike knew that as long as she was on his side, his father wouldn't object. He gave a loud shout and, grabbing Beetlejuice off his shoulders, did a little dance, holding the skunk tight against his body. "You're better'n a rabbit's foot," he cried. "I'd rather have you than a million four-leaf clovers."

The skunk yawned, showing a row of sharp white teeth, then winked one bright eye at him as though to say, "Just call on me whenever the going gets rough, Pal."

Chapter

3

*I*t took Mike a month to build the space hut, working every afternoon after school and on weekends. To keep Beetlejuice from getting in the way, he tied him on a long rope, letting him stay near enough to watch but not near enough to clamber up his legs and crawl into the favorite position around his neck. Who ever heard of anyone building a space hut with a skunk wrapped around his shoulders? The small animal ambled about the yard, happy as long as it was near Mike. It spent the time digging for insects or rolling onto its back and lying motionless in the warm spring sunshine.

"When I get it finished," Mike promised his pet, "I'll

take you up there. Maybe some night I'll even show you the star you were named after."

By April the work was done and it seemed to Mike he had been up and down the tree at least a million times, carrying lumber one piece at a time, going back for hammer and nails, then back for more lumber over and over and over again. When he had nailed the last board step to the trunk, he asked his father to come outside. His mother had watched its progress, day by day.

"There it is," Mike announced proudly.

His father stood under the tree and looked up. "Seems mighty high. Are you sure those boards are solid enough for steps? Are you sure the hut won't blow down when the first wind comes along? Are you positive you've built it strong and sturdy enough?"

Mike grinned. He knew lawyers were used to asking questions, that his father wasn't criticizing it even if it sounded that way. "Why not go up and inspect it, Dad?" he suggested. "Why not look for yourself, check it out and see if I did a good job?"

His father shook his head. "I'm not as young as I used to be. Anyway, I haven't the time now. Too much to do. I'll have to take your word for it." He seemed a little worried as he measured the tree's height with his eyes. "I just hope your mother and I weren't too hasty in giving you permission to build it. Don't you go falling out of it," he ordered, starting to leave. Seeing the look on his son's face, he added, "Besides, I couldn't climb a tree in my best suit, now could I?"

Mike was disappointed. He had counted so much on showing his father the inside of the hut, showing how well he had planned it and how carefully he had built it. He wanted him to climb up to it and know the same feeling he had when he was up there, of endless space around him, of how near the sky seemed, of how astronauts must feel in their capsules.

He didn't say anything to his friends at school right away, even though the hut was ready now for visitors. He wanted a few days to enjoy it alone, sitting up there after school, his feet dangling over the edge of the side he had left open as an entrance and so that he might see the houses and yards below, the river that twisted away and lost itself in the hills. Now he could watch each new leaf as it appeared on the tree, greet the robins as they returned from the south, boldly curious to find their tree occupied. He took his schoolbooks up with him, but he got very little studying done. There was always too much to watch, too much to see, too much to dream about up there.

He took Beetlejuice up too and the little animal strolled about the hut leisurely in its flat-footed way, inspecting every corner. Its small bright eyes watched the robins hungrily, its plumed tail waving back and forth.

One afternoon, not long after finishing the hut, he burst into the house after school to find his mother waiting for him in the front hall. The skunk as usual was waiting too and with a leap was up his leg and arm and onto his shoulders, nuzzling his neck and digging its claws into his school jacket.

From the look on his mother's face, Mike could see that something was wrong. What was it, he wondered. Had he forgotten to put the power mower away last night? Had he left it out in the rain again? He laid his books carefully on the table beside the door instead of tossing them onto the chair as he usually did.

"Michael, the hut has to come down!"

His mother's words stunned him. It was as though someone had struck him a paralyzing blow. He stared at her, not understanding. Her hands were clasped together tightly and he could tell this was as unpleasant for her as it was for him.

"Come down?" he repeated.

"Or be torn down," she said. "A man was here today from the Building Inspector's office."

Rebellion surged through Mike. Clenching his fists, he forced himself to speak as calmly as he could. "Why?"

"I'll tell you all I know," she answered. "A man came to the door a while ago, and as near as I can remember, he said, 'Whoever put that eyesore in the top of the big tree in your back yard should get rid of it right away, Ma'am. If not, the Building Inspector will have to have it torn down. Because you people are new in town, you'll be given the chance to take care of this yourself; otherwise there'll be a crew sent out to do it.' "

Mike looked at her in horror. The man had called his brand-new beautiful hut an "eyesore"? The hut he had built with such pains after so much planning? He couldn't believe it.

His mother went on, "It seems the recently appointed City Manager has been getting complaints about unsightly property in the city and when he was out looking around the other day, he happened to see your hut. The man who came today said the City Manager, Mr. Drake, believes that it isn't fair for people who work hard and save their money in order to live in a nice section like this to have to look at such a thing. So, it will have to come down."

Mike listened in shocked bewilderment. "But the leaves will be out in a few more weeks and nobody will see it then," he cried. He knew she was only repeating what the man had told her, that her heart ached for him as she explained it. "It isn't fair to me," he said. "Did Mr. Drake ever think of that?"

His mother seemed to be struggling to keep her voice steady. "Michael, I'm trying to see his side of this too. He's new here and he's only doing his duty, only doing what he was hired to do."

"Is this City Manager the head of the city?" Mike asked. "Who says he has the right to tell me what to do with my hut?"

"The City Manager is supposed to run the city so everyone will enjoy living in it. He has a campaign on now to improve its appearance and he's asking people to paint their houses, repair their fences, keep their lawns trimmed. And he's asking us to get rid of the hut."

"But is he the head of the city?" Mike insisted.

She looked at him sympathetically, sharing his disappointment. "No. There's a council and the members of it appoint him, but it is his job to improve the city in any way he can. We can't go against him, Mike."

It seemed to him then that she was letting him down, taking sides against him. Without lifting Beetlejuice off his shoulders, he rushed through the kitchen, out the back door, and to the foot of the oak tree. He wouldn't cry. He wouldn't! Beetlejuice hung on frantically, his claws digging into Mike's clothes.

Mike pressed his fingers into the rough bark until they tingled with pain but it didn't help. He put his foot on the first step and started to climb. If he was going to bawl like a baby, he'd do it up there in the hut where no one could see him.

The hut above him shook gently in the stirring wind. Halfway up, a black despair came over Mike and he stopped and pressed his face into the deep-rutted trunk.

"It's mine!" he said aloud. "I won't let them tear it down. I won't." How could he stop them? Could he and Beetlejuice go up there after stocking the hut with food and water and refuse to come down? Could he take the steps away and not let anyone come up until the leaves were out and the hut hidden? Would it work? Even while he asked himself such questions, he knew it wouldn't. His father would simply come to the foot of the tree and shout in a loud voice, "Michael, come down at once!" and what could he do then but go down?

The hut began to rock now, as though it were alive. Birds flew out of the top of the tree, scolding as they left. Mike watched, curious. The wind wasn't that strong.

He started up the steps again, keeping an eye on the hut. Suddenly two dungaree-clad legs and a pair of sneakers appeared over the edge of the hut's platform and swung idly in the air.

Someone had discovered his hut! Someone was sitting up there acting as though he owned it.

An unreasonable anger seized Mike. All the disappointment and rage and heartbreak he had felt since his mother told him the hut had to be torn down turned now upon the trespasser sitting up there in his hut. He clutched the tree to steady himself. Twisting his head around, he tried to see who belonged to the legs, but from his position beneath the platform he couldn't get a glimpse of the body above. He ran up the remaining board steps and as he approached, the sneakers disappeared. Pulling the top half of himself into the doorway while his feet remained on the last step, Mike peered into the hut.

Chapter

4

*I*n a corner of the space hut, jackknifed snugly where the walls joined, was a small figure.

"Come in!" a thin reedy voice commanded. "Don't just hang there, half-in and half-out. Come in, boy."

Still angry, Mike pulled himself into the hut. Whoever this was had a lot of nerve, ordering him to come into his own hut. He seated himself on the opposite side and looked at the intruder. Not much larger than Mike was himself, a little old man sat there, a man seventy years old at least. Edging his face was a border of neatly trimmed white whiskers, and his eyes were as black and bright as Beetlejuice's. In his right hand was a knife he had been using to pare the outer bark from a small branch. Shavings lay on his lap and on the surrounding floor. Before Mike could say a word, the old man shifted the knife to his left hand and pointed a finger at the animal on his shoulders.

"Genus *Mephitis mephitis*," he said, "commonly known as North American skunk. Make wonderful pets, I've heard. What's its name?"

"Beetlejuice," Mike answered, his anger beginning to fade. He had forgotten the skunk was still clinging to him.

"Let's see," the stranger said, cocking his head to one side. "That's the giant red star, isn't it? Near one shoulder of Orion." He grinned and, reaching out, stroked the animal's shiny coat. "Your name Orion, boy? Seems this Beetlejuice stays mighty close to your shoulder too."

Mike was surprised. Most people didn't want anything to do with a skunk. Most people didn't know one star from another either.

The old man nodded his head toward his surroundings. "It's a fine hut. Could stand a wee bit more bracing perhaps. Just enough to make it good and steady in a high wind. That open side could be closed up so you'd be nice and cosy up here in bad weather. I've been studying how to do it. If you put hinges at the top, you could raise and lower the side wall as you saw fit."

Mike was pulled two ways. He didn't like a stranger who had invited himself up into the hut criticizing it, yet he knew in his heart that what this man was saying was right. His solution to the problem was a good one.

"You've done a real shipshape job," the trespasser

continued, waving the knife in a circle to take in the whole structure. "Yes, it's as fine a hut as I've ever seen and I've seen a lot in my day."

The words pleased Mike, the first praise he had received from someone who had been up and seen the hut first-hand. "Who are you?" he asked, settling himself against the wall and staring at the man. "What are you doing here?"

The old man's laugh was thin and high. "I didn't see a keep-out sign anywhere. And since I used to be a tree hut builder myself, I couldn't resist the urge to visit yours." He smiled. "I watched you put it together, boy. Watched you build the whole thing." Leaning his head back on the wall, he gazed at Mike. "Who am I? Why, just someone who can't help admiring a good piece of workmanship when he sees one. Call me Mr. Moon."

With a gesture so quick that the boy instinctively drew back, he thrust out his hand. "I'd be proud to be your friend. I didn't know there were boys left who had imagination and skill enough to plan and build something like this. Or the patience. Seems everything moves along so fast nowadays."

Mike looked at the outstretched hand. It was old, as gnarled and twisted as the branches of the oak tree, but it was steady and friendly. He relaxed and put out his hand and they shook. "My name is Mike McAllister," he said. There was a moment of silence then, as though to mark the beginning of their friendship.

This man knew about tree huts and had built them

himself, Mike was thinking. And he had said he'd watched the building of this one, which proved he really was interested. The most amazing thing was that he had climbed all the way up here at his age, to look the hut over. Gesturing toward the board steps, Mike asked, "Have any trouble getting up those?"

Mr. Moon looked surprised. "I'm not as young as I used to be, boy, but I don't allow my years to keep me from doing whatever I set out to do." He shrugged. "Most of this age business is in your mind anyway."

"I'm not as young as I used to be," were exactly the words Mike's father had used, and Mr. Moon must be twice his age. "I wanted my dad to come up here," Mike admitted, "but he didn't. He didn't have time."

Mr. Moon waved a hand in the air as though he were waving away Mike's disappointment. "Don't let it worry you. There are some mighty fine people who never seem to have time to take time to enjoy life." He chuckled. "It's not their fault. They really believe that if they take their finger off the button, the world will stop turning." Grinning, he added, "You'll see. I'll bet when your dad's a little older he'll relax and want to do all the things he didn't have time for before. You probably won't be able to keep him out of here then."

Suddenly Mike remembered. The surprise of finding Mr. Moon in the hut had driven the Building Inspector's order right out of his mind. Now, his awful despair returned.

"It won't be here then," he said. "It won't even be here next month. It's going to be torn down."

It seemed as if Mr. Moon hadn't heard him. He didn't say anything, just took up the knife again and whittled away at the branch in his hand. He didn't seem to be trying to make any certain thing, just stripped the last trace of bark from the branch, leaving it white and smooth and slightly moist. Then he laid down the knife, sighed a long contented sigh, and folded his arms over his chest.

Beetlejuice, rousing from a nap on Mike's shoulders, jumped to the hut floor, strolled across it and crouched at the edge of the platform, his eyes on a bird preening itself on a nearby branch.

"Want to talk about it?" Mr. Moon asked Mike.

Mike did want to talk about it, to talk with someone who knew how he felt, who knew how important a tree hut could be to the one who had built it. Mr. Moon was just the right person to talk to.

He opened his mouth and the words rushed out like a river breaking through a dam. He told about the crating and how he had come by it, about drawing his plans and getting his parents' consent to build. He told about calling it a space hut and how he meant to have his friends come up and share it with him. He explained how someday all of them meant to travel in space and this could be a kind of beginning for them.

"I put it all together myself." He pointed to the roof of the hut, to the walls, the floor. "I can't take it apart

34 33 34

now. Gee, you'd think this was one of those countries where they tell you what to do whether it's right or not." His voice grew shaky and he had to wait a minute before going on. "And I don't see how anyone could call it an eyesore. I think it looks great." He wondered if maybe that wasn't what had hurt the most, having someone call it that when he had worked so hard to make it neat as well as sturdy.

Mr. Moon listened but he didn't interrupt. He didn't even say anything when Mike finished and slumped back against the wall. Instead, he searched through his pockets and finally found what he was looking for. It turned out to be two licorice sticks, and he offered one to the boy.

"Never could get enough licorice when I was young," he said as he bit off a large piece. The skunk sniffed, wiggled his nose, got up and came to Mr. Moon, his eyes on the sticky black candy. Mike held his and looked at it. Just like a grown-up, he was thinking. Mr. Moon acted interested in the hut but he was just like the rest, giving you a piece of candy to make everything all right. He raised his eyes and glared at the old man.

Mr. Moon, watching, shook his head. "I'm not trying to bribe you to forget your troubles," he said. "Not trying to make light of them either because they're real enough all right. I just wanted a little thinking time." Somehow that made Mike feel better, and he watched the old man break off a small piece, put it on the floor for Beetlejuice, and chew the rest slowly. When he finished, he wiped his hands on his clean dungarees.

"What do you know about the history of tree huts, boy? Have you done your homework on them?"

Mike blinked. What did that have to do with tearing his hut down? "I guess I don't know anything about that," he admitted. "Should I?"

"Of course. When you're interested in something, you ought to take the time to find out everything there is to know about it. People have been building tree huts ever since the world began. Some of our primitive ancestors worshipped trees because that was where they believed their gods lived. Trees fed, clothed, and sheltered the first men. They offered protection from floods and wild animals and from everything threatening on the ground. Trees were the first refuge our ancestors knew."

Mike found himself listening hard to what the old man was saying. "I didn't know that," he said.

"Right now in the Philippine Islands, whole villages are built right in trees. Did you know that?" Mr. Moon asked. "They even have bridge paths from tree to tree so the natives don't have to come down until they want to." Mr. Moon was warming up to the subject. His eyes sparkled and Mike guessed it was one of his favorite topics. "I've seen them," he said. "I've even been up in them."

Beetlejuice, delighted with the taste of the licorice, squeaked for more. Mr. Moon lifted him up and placed him upon his own shoulders and the skunk winked a beady eye at Mike. Then, playfully, he reached down and buried his face in the white whiskers.

"And in Africa," the old man went on, smiling, "some of the natives build huts that look just like beehives. They fix them to the branches of the baobab tree. Sometimes thirty families live in one tree, so you can imagine how big it is."

He leaned back and shook his head. "There I go again. Can't stop once I get started. But I did want you to know about this so you would understand there are a lot more reasons for building tree huts than for tearing them down."

"But they're going to tear mine down," Mike said, "reasons or not."

He wasn't sure if Mr. Moon really said it but he thought he heard the words, "Not if you put up a good fight." When he looked at the old man, he realized he must have imagined it, for Mr. Moon seemed to have exhausted himself. He was sound asleep, his whiskers moving gently with his breathing, the branch held loosely between his relaxed fingers. Beetlejuice slept along with him, his head tucked under the whiskers, his plumed tail barely moving to and fro.

Chapter 5

*T*hat night at dinner, the hut was discussed at the table. Mike hoped his father would have some suggestions on what he could do to keep it, and he waited anxiously to hear what he had to say. His father was a lawyer and he would know.

"I guess it will have to come down," his mother said. "The man who came here told me it was the City Manager himself who gave the order."

Mike looked at his father, his last hope.

Mr. McAllister shifted uncomfortably in his chair. "Son, I know you're disappointed after putting so much work into your hut, but I'm afraid there's nothing we can do."

The words struck Mike like a gust of icy wind, taking his breath away.

"You know, I'm just setting up my law practice here," his father continued, "and I can't start off in a new place by getting into a fight with the city officials. The hut just isn't important enough to risk losing me goodwill in this town when I need it most."

"But . . ." Mike began.

His father shook his head. "I don't want to talk about it any more because there's nothing I can do. If it has to come down, then it will come down and that's all there is to it. You can rebuild it on the ground where it will be a lot safer."

"On the ground?" Mike repeated, shocked. His father just didn't understand. A space hut on the ground wouldn't make any sense at all.

Mr. McAllister got up and laid his napkin beside his plate. "There's a lesson in this for you, son. A good American works for and with his community, for the good of the most people. Sometimes one person has to give up what he wants for the good of everyone. If you don't understand that now, someday you will."

Mike didn't say anything. He looked at his mother. She surely understood why the hut had to be up there in the top of the oak tree. She knew you couldn't have a space hut on the ground and he hoped she would explain it to his father. But she only smiled consolingly across the table. He knew then that she couldn't help him either.

"How do we get it down?" his father asked. "Do you want me to help you take it out of the tree?"

"No, George," his mother said quickly, "don't make him do it. If the Building Inspector wants it down, let him arrange to have someone take it down. That man said they would send a crew out to do it if we didn't and I think it's up to them. It's just too much to expect of Mike, having him undo all his work right after he's finished it."

His father threw up his hands. "All right, all right. Let them send men out then. I guess they need work and this will give them some."

Mike went to his room and lay on the bed, thinking. He hadn't mentioned Mr. Moon to his parents. Maybe his mother would think the old man was a tramp and shouldn't be hanging around. Maybe his father would even order him off their property. It would be hard to explain that Mr. Moon was his friend even though he didn't know anything about him. How did you explain someone who just appeared out of nowhere and didn't say where he'd come from or where he belonged? Mr. Moon was the only one besides himself who really cared about the hut, who understood why someone would climb to a tree hut and stay up there for hours, just dreaming and pretending and planning.

What was it he thought the old man had said? "Not if you put up a good fight." If Mr. Moon had really said it, why had he gone to sleep without explaining what he meant? What kind of fight could a boy put up when his father, who was a lawyer, said nothing could be done about it?

The outside air was cold and Mike got up to close the window. He looked at the oak tree, wondering if Mr. Moon could still be up there in the hut. He hadn't thought to ask him if he had somewhere to stay. Somehow you just didn't ask Mr. Moon questions like that. You waited until he told you what he wanted you to know. But now the thought worried the boy. Suppose the old man didn't have anywhere else to go, suppose he didn't have anything to eat?

Mike tiptoed downstairs and looked into the kitchen. His mother was busy washing the dishes and he knew he couldn't take Mr. Moon food without explaining it to her. She caught sight of him peering around the hall door.

"Better get to bed, Mike. I'll say goodnight now instead of coming up later. I have an evening's work ahead of me, cleaning out this refrigerator and freezer."

He went back upstairs again, still worried about the old man. Tomorrow I'll take him a pillow and blanket, he decided. If he wants to, he can sleep in the hut until they come to tear it down. I'll take him something to eat too. There wouldn't be much he could take without explaining, but that would be all right. Mr. Moon was such a little old man that he probably didn't eat very much anyway.

Before he went to sleep he remembered that his father had said, "I don't want to talk about it any more because there's nothing I can do." He hadn't said Mike shouldn't do anything. This left him free to act if he could just think of something to do. Instead of going to sleep, he began to go over and over ideas in his mind. At last he felt he had hit upon one that was worth trying. On Saturday the new playground near the school was to be dedicated, his teacher had announced and told the class, "Four of our city councilmen will be there and the public is invited."

Maybe he could get to talk to the councilmen and tell them about his hut. He could ask them to change the Building Inspector's order. Since his father wouldn't do anything about the hut, he would go to the dedication alone. His mother had told him the City Manager was appointed by the Council. He might as well start right at the top.

It was getting so that Mike was so used to Beetlejuice lying across his shoulders that he hardly noticed the animal. Sometimes when the skunk dug his claws into a shoulder, Mike was surprised to find him there. Without thinking twice about it, he started off for the playground on Saturday with his pet clinging to his jacket collar. When he reached the area he saw it was already crowded. There was a small platform in place with a loudspeaker set up on it.

Figuring that the best time to see the councilmen would be as they arrived before the ceremony began, he sat down on a curb where a parking section had been reserved, the sign reading "Officials Only." Beetlejuice lay like a fur collar upon his shoulders, fast asleep.

After what seemed like a long time, a car drew up to the curb. Four men were inside and Mike knew the time had come to speak up for his hut. Getting to his feet, he waited until the councilmen, laughing and talking to each other, got out of the car. When they were standing together on the sidewalk, he approached, meaning to explain everything quickly so he could get it all said before they started across the playground to where the crowd waited.

He had just opened his mouth to begin when one of the officials, seeing Mike there with Beetlejuice curled about his neck, stopped laughing and pointed. "Glory be, it's a skunk!" he shouted. "On my last hunting trip I tangled with one of them and the fellows made me set up a separate camp for the next three days."

"He's tame," Mike said, stepping forward. "I wanted to ask if anyone has the right to . . ."

"Tame or not," another called out, backing away, "just don't bring that animal within firing distance of me. I know what it can do. I was brought up in the mountains and I've seen those varmints operate. Seen them shoot six shots in succession and hit a bull's-eye at ten paces."

"But he . . . he can't . . . he . . . won't . . ." His stuttering prevented Mike from telling them how harmless the skunk was. By this time the men were moving across the playground and he was trailing them, trying to explain.

"Haven't run a race in years," a fat councilman wheezed to the others, "but I'll bet I can get out of here faster than any of the rest of you."

To Mike's amazement, all four took off, their coats flapping behind them, their legs stretched and running. It didn't seem to him very dignified for city councilmen to arrive red in the face and out of breath at a dedication ceremony.

He stopped and watched them go. There was no use following, since he already knew what kind of welcome he would get with Beetlejuice around his neck. The skunk, however, didn't seem to be at all concerned about the furor he had created. He just shook his feathery tail, dug his claws a little deeper into Mike's shoulder, squeaked happily, then solemnly winked one small bright eye at his owner.

"Big help you turned out to be," Mike grumbled, turning for home.

Chapter

6

It took Mike through Sunday and Monday to get over his failure with the city councilmen. He blamed himself for having taken Beetlejuice with him. Next time he'd be smarter.

On Monday night while he was doing his homework, it occurred to him that if he could point out to the Building Inspector that once the leaves were on the oak tree neither the City Manager nor anyone else would be able to see the hut, maybe everything would be all right. Maybe no one had thought of that.

He could go to town right from school tomorrow. Getting home late wouldn't matter since his mother would be attending a PTA meeting. He found he didn't want to talk about his efforts to keep the hut. If he was successful, it would be time enough to explain what he had done.

Going downstairs, he looked in the phone book under City Offices and found the address of the Building Inspector's office. He wrote it down, then went to bed, hopeful that he had at last hit upon the best solution.

When he arrived at the right corridor and the right room in the municipal office building the next day, he found a sign reading "ENTER" upon the door. Cautiously, he peered in. The room was empty. He hesitated for a moment, then took a few steps in and looked around. It was a large untidy dark room with an old-fashioned high ceiling. A desk by the window was piled high with papers and booklets and printed charts. Over everything lay a coat of dust which, disturbed now by the draft from the open door, rose in a small cloud. Mike sneezed.

At once the door to an inner office flew open and a big man appeared in the doorway.

"Well," he said, "it's about time. Where's the paper?"

Mike looked at him, puzzled. "What paper, sir?"

"The newspaper." The look on the boy's face answered for him so the man threw back his head and laughed. "Guess you aren't the newsboy."

"No, sir."

"Good thing for you, I guess. I was about to give you a bad time. I haven't had a newspaper for the last two days and I was all ready and waiting to pounce on that delivery boy."

Mike went back and shut the door. "I just came to see the Building Inspector," he explained.

Surprise showed on the man's face. "To see me? What's your problem? Want a new room added to your house or a swimming pool to your yard?" Assuming a business-like expression, he stepped to his desk and motioned Mike to a chair beside it.

Sitting gingerly on the edge of it, Mike studied the man. He was so heavy that the chair creaked beneath his weight, so big that the regular-sized desk in front of him seemed too small. Smile wrinkles showed at the corners of his eyes.

Mike didn't feel uneasy any longer. He liked the man's looks. "I want to keep my tree hut, sir. My space hut."

The big man again seemed surprised. "Don't your folks want you to keep it?" he asked.

"Oh, they said I could. They let me build it."

"Well," said the Inspector, "if they aren't worried about you falling out of the tree, why don't you keep it?"

Mike was growing confused. "Because it's going to be torn down."

The Building Inspector was even more confused. "Why?"

Mike wondered if the man was making fun of him. If so, it wasn't a very good joke, he decided, looking at the Inspector accusingly. "You know why. Because you said it had to be."

The oversized man was so startled that he threw himself back in his chair, causing it to creak loudly. "I did not!" he protested. "I like tree huts, space huts, whatever you call them. If more boys built huts in trees today the police wouldn't have to be running them off the streets. What kind of tree is it in?"

Mike didn't see why that mattered. "An oak."

The Inspector smiled broadly. "An oak tree," he said, shaking his head as though the words brought back a flood of memories. "I had a hut in an oak tree when I was young. Used to take my lunch up there on Saturday and spend the whole day in my hut. Why, my dog used to go crazy waiting for me to come down. He'd howl like a . . ." He sat forward and looked at Mike. "Who told you I said it had to be torn down?"

"My mother said so. A man from your office came to our house and said he had an order from you to tear the hut down if we don't do it ourselves."

The Inspector put his chin in his large hand and drew his heavy brows together. He sat there scowling for a few minutes, then suddenly leaped out of his chair and went into the other office. The old wooden floor shook beneath his feet. Mike could hear him talking to someone and when he returned, he held a piece of paper in his hand.

"I give you my word of honor," he said, "cross my heart and hope to die, I didn't know anything about it. My secretary says the order came from the City Manager while I was away at a meeting last week. No one told me about it when I got back."

It was plain that he was annoyed. He looked around, then leaned across the desk and spoke in a low voice. "The City Manager's new here and you know what they say about a new broom sweeping clean. I hear he's been all over the city, poking into everything. Our last City Manager was an old fellow who didn't stir things up, just let things take care of themselves mostly. But this one's young and . . ." He swung his chair around and looked out the window. Mike could see a red flush creeping up the back of his neck.

The Building Inspector's next words were angry and spoken in a loud voice. "He's got no right to be sending my men out on silly errands like that."

Suddenly he swung around and his fist smashed the desk with such a powerful blow that it jumped and shivered. Mike decided the Building Inspector had a king-sized temper. "By golly," the big man said, "I won't just sit here and let him get away with it. If I do this time, no telling what he'll try next. I'm going to speak my mind . . ."

Mike watched as he dialed a number on the phone and asked to speak to the City Manager.

"Mr. Drake?" he said when he finally got through. "This is Charlie Monahan, Building Inspector. I just found out about that tree hut you want torn down."

There were impatient sounds from the receiver.

"Wait a minute, wait a minute," Mr. Monahan said loudly. "Okay, you're busy, but at least tell me why you're picking on kids. Sure, there's a need to clean up the city but why not start by burning off weeds on some of those empty lots or tearing down those old firetraps on East Street. Now those are really eyesores. Some of them have been standing empty for the last ten years or more."

He listened, then spoke again. "What harm is a kid's tree hut doing? Those old warehouses are dangerous. If you want to get all het up about something, get het up about them."

The voice coming over the wire was just as angry as Charlie Monahan's. Listening, the Inspector drummed his fingers on the desk, his mouth thinned into a stubborn line. Finally he looked like he couldn't stand it any longer.

"Hold on," he shouted. "I won't do it! I've been running my office for eight years without complaints from anyone. Don't tell me to go out and tear down a kid's tree hut because I won't, and I've got good reasons. You just hang on and I'll tell you . . ."

Mike's heart leaped. The Inspector was taking his side.

The voice coming out of the receiver cut into Mr. Monahan's sentence; then there was a loud bang. The man at the desk looked startled.

"What did he say?" Mike asked anxiously.

The Building Inspector's face had gone blank, as though he couldn't believe what he had heard.

"What did he say?" Mike asked again.

Charlie Monahan spoke like a man in a daze. "He says he's going to suspend me. He's sending me written notice."

Chapter 7

*M*ike ate his apple at lunch the next day at school but set his sandwiches aside. After school he would take them to the hut for Mr. Moon. He had left the blanket and pillow there yesterday when he got home from town but there had been no sign of the old man.

When Mike reached the hut, Mr. Moon was sitting cross-legged on the floor with his head against the wall and his eyes closed. His knife was in his hand and today there was a new branch, the bark half stripped away. Mike didn't feel much like grinning, but he couldn't help it when he saw this picture of perfect contentment. It was good to know Mr. Moon loved the hut as much as he did.

Outside a spring wind rattled the tree limbs, but here inside there was protection and snug comfort. As Mike settled himself against the opposite wall, Mr. Moon opened one eye slowly and sighed with happiness.

"Greetings," he said, "I see Beetlejuice is still right in place, on the shoulder of Orion."

Undoing the wrappings, Mike placed the sandwiches on the floor beside the little old man. "It's a kind of picnic," he said. "I hope you like peanut butter and jelly. I saved them from my lunch."

The sandwiches looked a little smashed, with the grape jelly oozing out, but the old man looked at them as though they were a feast. Mike shoved them closer. "Save them till later if you want to," he said, thinking perhaps the old man wouldn't want him to see how hungry he was.

Mr. Moon gathered them up and held them as though they were rare and precious. "I've never been offered finer hospitality in my life," he said in a voice reedier than usual. "Knowing you did without so you could bring them to me . . ." He blinked. "And thanks for the pillow and blanket." He didn't say whether he had used them or not.

A silence fell between them, the comfortable kind that makes old friends feel closer. A robin, plump and orange-breasted, settled on a nearby branch. Its button-round eyes watched them curiously. Mr. Moon, pursing his lips, made bird sounds and the robin cocked its head to one side. Beetlejuice roused himself and stared.

"None of that," Mr. Moon cautioned the skunk. "There'll be no robins for a snack today." To Mike he said, "Used to be able to sweet talk them right into my tree hut when I was a boy. Used to know all sorts of bird calls. Could fool them every time."

Mike tried to imagine Mr. Moon as a boy. He must have looked just as he did right now, except for the whiskers, the boy decided.

"Anything new?" the old man asked.

Mike told him about going to the Inspector's office. "I liked him but he couldn't help me. Maybe I shouldn't have gone. The City Manager got so mad at him, he's going to fire him, I think, and it was all my fault."

"Fire him?" Mr. Moon asked. "I didn't think a City Manager had that power."

"It sure sounded that way." Mike thought a minute. "No, I guess what he said was he would suspend the Inspector."

"Have you talked to your father about keeping the hut?"

Mike flushed. "He's an awfully good citizen," he said loyally. "He says you should do what you're told to do when it's for the good of the most people."

Mr. Moon nodded. "And he's right. The City Manager has the job of running the city and its citizens are supposed to help him do it."

Mike's morale sagged. He was getting more and more discouraged by the minute. "Then I guess there's nothing I can do. I'll just have to let them tear the hut down."

The old man laid aside the branch he was whittling on. "Hold on there, boy. What your father said was right IF, for instance, the City Manager was getting rid of unsightly property that bothers a lot of people. If you don't believe such a description fits your hut, you'd better stand up for your rights."

Mike thought it over. "You mean I ought to fight back when something isn't fair?"

Mr. Moon nodded. "I do." Then he pulled his knees up under his chin so that he looked like a jack-in-the-box, ready to leap if someone pressed the catch. "Mike, don't ever forget that our Constitution guarantees us all life, liberty, and the pursuit of happiness."

Mike felt a new stir of hope. "We're studying the Constitution in history class now," he said. "I wish I could talk to my father about this. Maybe if I told him what you said, he could think of something to do." He thought over what he'd said, then frowned. "It wouldn't work. He won't talk about the hut, so I'd better not bring it up again."

Mr. Moon shot up suddenly as though that spring had indeed been released. "Sometimes a man has to fight his own fight," he said and before Mike could answer, he was off down the tree like a squirrel that had just spied a prize acorn on the ground below.

Because the teachers were to attend a meeting, Thursday was a school holiday and Mike and Beetlejuice went to the hut right after breakfast. Mr. Moon was sitting as usual in a corner and as usual he was clean and neat, his dungarees pressed and his shirt spotless. Mike wondered again if he would ever find out the truth about the little old man. Who was he and where did he live? He had to admit to himself that now what mattered most was just having him for a friend, having him here to talk to, to listen to. Yes sir, he told himself, the best you could wish anybody with problems was that he could have a Mr. Moon on his side.

Beetlejuice, on his way to settle down at the edge of the platform and watch the birds, nuzzled the old man and Mr. Moon gazed at him fondly, trailing a finger down the white stripe on the side of the skunk's thick black coat.

His eyes shining with excitement, Mike reached in his pocket and brought out a piece of blank paper and a fountain pen. He laid them on the hut floor.

"I had a great idea. I remembered last night that when we lived in that apartment in the city, a lady came around one day with a petition for my Mom to sign. She said it would keep the owner from raising the rent if everyone signed it. She read it out loud."

Mr. Moon smiled. "Did it keep the rent down?"

Mike shrugged. "I don't know. We moved right after that, but I thought maybe if I wrote a petition and took it around and asked people in the neighborhood to sign it, it might help me keep my hut. If enough people sign, it would show the City Manager that everybody doesn't think my hut is an eyesore and that there's no good reason to tear it down."

Mr. Moon smacked his hands together, scaring a loud squeak out of Beetlejuice. "Splendid!" he cried. "That's using your head. Now, what do you plan to say in it?"

Mike hesitated. "I thought maybe you'd . . ."

"Help? Of course I'll help, but first I'd like to hear your idea."

Mike dug into his pocket again and brought out a folded paper. "I made some notes last night. Copied them out of my history book."

Mr. Moon nodded. "Let's hear them."

"In the chapter on the Constitution, under Amendments, Article IV, it says 'The right of the people to be secure in their persons, houses, papers, and effects against unreasonable searches and seizures . . .'" He stopped. "Is tearing down a hut the same as seizing it? I figured it could be."

Mr. Moon pondered, tugging at his whiskers. "I'd say it was. And you couldn't find a better authority than the Constitution. Good for you for thinking of that."

It had been Mr. Moon's bringing up the Constitution yesterday that had given Mike the idea of searching it to find what he needed, but anyone listening now would think it was Mike who had thought of it all by himself, who had discovered the Constitution as surely as Columbus had discovered America.

Mr. Moon picked up the pen and crossed out a few words. "'The right of the people to be secure in their houses against unreasonable seizures.' Getting rid of those few extra words will make it clearer," he said, "and it

doesn't change the meaning one bit."

Mike had a sudden thought. " 'People' doesn't mean just grown-ups, does it?"

The little old man's voice rang through the hut and Beetlejuice, disturbed again, leaped to his feet, waving his tail angrily from side to side. "People is everyone," Mr. Moon shouted. "Little or big, young or old, black, white, yellow, or red. You name anybody and he's a people. That's what's so wonderful about the word." He held out the branch he had been working on. "See this? It's just like people. Strip off the outside layer and you'll find them all the same underneath."

Mike grinned. When his friend believed something, he believed it loud and hard. Mr. Moon now placed the paper in front of him and took up the pen. "You say it and I'll write it."

Just then Mike heard his mother's voice. For a minute he was afraid she had heard Mr. Moon shouting and had come to ask who was up there in the hut with him. He peered down to see her crossing the yard.

"Mike, that man was here again," she called. "He came to see what we are going to do about getting rid of the hut. I told him we'd decided to let them send a crew out and he said one would be here before the end of the month. I thought you'd want to know."

"That's okay, Mom," Mike said, his voice cheerful as he looked down at her from the hut platform. Waving, he pulled himself back into the building, but not before he saw that she was looking up at him in open-mouthed surprise at his reaction to the news.

Beetlejuice leaped on his arm and settled himself on Mike's shoulders. "Now, where did we leave off? Oh, yes . . . that petition I told you about started 'I, the under-signed,'. I guess that's all I remember about it."

"Let's start it that way then," Mr. Moon said and, hunching himself over the paper, wrote the words carefully. "What comes next?"

"I, the undersigned, believe an American boy . . ."

"Fine. Keep going."

". . . has the right to plan and build and . . ." Mike was stuck. He searched unsuccessfully for a word.

"Occupy?" Mr. Moon suggested.

". . . occupy a space hut on his own father's property without having to worry about unreasonable seizure."

Mr. Moon wrote and then waited. "That all?" he finally asked.

Mike wrinkled his forehead. "I guess so," he said. "Is it enough? It seems to say everything that's important."

The old man looked up from the paper and smiled. "There are very few people who know when to stop writing, or talking. I'd say it was just fine."

Mr. Moon's letters had flowed from his pen, tall and graceful, with sweeping curls and flourishes. He wrote slowly and carefully, dotting an "i" here, crossing a "t" there with artistic strokes and shadings.

"Gee!" Mike cried. "That's great! It looks just like the writing on the Bill of Rights hanging on the wall of our history room at school."

Mr. Moon held the paper at arm's length and examined it. "In a way that's what this is," he declared. "A boy's Bill of Rights to be free to dream his dreams and enjoy the work of his hands."

When he was satisfied that the ink was dry, he handed it to Mike. "Here it is, boy. Ammunition! Can't fight a battle without it, and the more you've got, the better."

The noon whistle blew and Mike folded the petition. "Have to go to lunch now," he said. "I'll get started on the signatures this afternoon."

Mr. Moon reached into his pocket and brought out a small package. In it was a peanut butter and jelly sandwich. Beetlejuice leaped from Mike's shoulder and walked flat-footedly over to investigate.

"Oh, no, you don't," the old man said, holding his lunch out of reach. "Your master's about to take you down with him so I can stay on here and work on that robin a little more." He looked at the boy, grinning. "You were planning on taking him with you, weren't you, Mike? Without him around, I expect to talk that bird into coming right through that opening and sharing my meal with me."

Chapter

8

*A*fter lunch, Mike started his search for people to sign the petition. He left Beetlejuice in his room, settled on the window sill. The skunk's bright gaze was fixed on the oak tree and the robins that busily flitted in and out of its leafy cover.

The boy began three blocks from home, intending to work his way back to his own block. The bell went unanswered at the first house he approached. He stood waiting and hoping, but when no one came he turned away, disappointment stealing some of his confidence.

A very fat woman sat on the porch of the next house. She rocked and watched him as he came up the walk, clutching the petition tightly in his hand, going over in

his mind what he intended to say. Taking the paper, she listened as he talked and when he finished rolled back her head and laughed until the tears streamed down her cheeks. Her large body shook convulsively, and Mike felt his face grow hot and his temper start to rise.

"I don't think it's funny," he said as politely as he could.

She took her handkerchief out of her pocket and wiped her eyes. "Now, don't go getting yourself in a huff. I'm laughing because I've waited so long for someone to do something about the way everyone pushes us taxpayers around. I never dreamed the only one with nerve enough to fight back would be a boy who wants to keep a hut he's built in a tree."

"Then you'll sign?"

"You bet I will." She took the pen and wrote her name across the paper. "Hmmmph! A campaign to clean up the city! He's a young one, this City Manager. Bet he's trying to make a name for himself fast. Probably means to get into state politics next. When you read about what all these eager beavers say they'll do, it sounds important. But how does it usually turn out? They just go out and order a boy's tree hut torn down. Talk big and act little, that's the way they do things."

Mike thanked her and edged away, wanting to get on with his signature collecting.

He was starting down the stairs when she called to him, "Good luck, Tiger. Stick to your guns. We need people who'll fight for what they believe."

He said goodbye and went on down the street, feeling good. He had the first signature! Going from door to door, he spoke his piece and hoped. People were kind and listened, but many of them refused to sign. He found one man who told him almost the same thing his father had, "Officials are paid to run the city and it's the good of most people they have to consider." He didn't sign.

Others pointed out that since a boy's tree hut wasn't a civic project, a city official had no right to interfere with it. They signed.

Some of the mothers turned him away, telling him they didn't hold with boys being encouraged to climb trees. "They can think up enough ways to get hurt without doing that." Or they said, "I wouldn't let my son risk his neck in a tree hut and I'm surprised your mother would."

The signature that meant the most belonged to an architect. After Mike had explained the petition to him, the man gave him an approving pat on the shoulder. "Good boy! Takes a lot of planning and work to build something. I know. I'll have to have a look at that hut myself, but right now I'd be honored to sign and help out a brother craftsman. Good luck!"

By five o'clock Mike had only twenty signatures. He hadn't thought to ask Mr. Moon how many he would need, but he felt sure twenty weren't enough. When he climbed the oak tree to tell his friend about it the old man had gone, so he sat up there alone for a long time, trying to talk himself out of his discouragement. If it hadn't been for Mr. Moon . . . There was something about the old man that wouldn't countenance the admission of failure. Yes, Mike told himself, he was lucky because if he could pick out just one friend when he needed him, he'd choose someone like Mr. Moon.

He sat through the evening meal in silence, speaking only when spoken to. His mother stopped and put her hand on his forehead as she went to the kitchen. He knew she was wondering if he could be sick because he was so quiet, but what was there to talk about? His father didn't want to hear about the hut and right now that was all that really mattered.

Before leaving the table he almost asked his parents to sign the petition. Two more names would be a help, but he decided against it. His father might not approve of it and his mother might say he shouldn't go around bothering the neighbors.

Up in his room he laid the petition on his desk and looked at it. To get enough signatures, he would probably have to cover half the city and he couldn't do that alone. There just wasn't time either to try to get his friends from school interested in helping. The deadline for the hut was approaching fast.

Desperate, he decided that maybe the twenty names could serve some purpose. They would at least show the City Manager how some people felt. If he could just talk to Mr. Drake it might help change his mind about the hut.

"I'll take the petition to him tomorrow," he said aloud to Beetlejuice. "I've got to do something . . . fast!"

Chapter

9

*W*hen Mike reached City Hall and found the right office the next day after school, he stood before the door in awe.

"OFFICE OF THE CITY MANAGER" was imprinted on the glass in imposing black letters. It had such a look of importance, of authority, that Mike felt his heart begin to thump and he backed off, waiting until he could muster the nerve to open the door. No one was in the corridor. He clenched his fists tightly and gave himself a pep talk, telling himself he couldn't back down now.

Carefully he turned the knob and opened the door just enough to allow himself to slip through, closing it silently. He looked around the office in surprise. There was a woman talking into a telephone at a desk in front of another door. On this one the lettering was in gold and read "ROGER DRAKE, CITY MANAGER."

His courage left him and he leaned back against the door. He had primed himself to face Mr. Drake but now it turned out he would have to get permission from the secretary in order to get through that other door. The woman was so busy she hadn't noticed him come in. Watching her, he saw there were worry wrinkles across her forehead and her eyebrows almost met in a frown. She snapped words into the instrument she held.

"No! No! No! Mr. Drake will be busy all afternoon. Call him next week. He couldn't possibly see you before then." With that she slammed the receiver into its cradle and turned back to her work.

Mike waited while she shuffled through a pile of papers and laid them aside. Then he pulled down his sweater the way his mother was always telling him to do, smoothed his hair, and stepped to the desk. The secretary looked up and gave a startled gasp.

"I didn't hear you," she said accusingly. "Why were you sneaking around like that?"

"I wasn't sneaking, Ma'am," Mike said.

She sighed impatiently. "Well, you can see I'm busy, can't you? What do you want?"

"I'd like . . . I'd like to see the City Manager."

She stared at him as though he were out of his mind. "Whatever for?"

Mike thought it over. He decided against telling his story twice so he said, "I just want to see him. It's private."

She pursed her thin lips. "Well, you can't! He's busy!" She gave a short little laugh. "Unless of course you have an appointment."

"No, Ma'am," Mike said.

She turned back to her work, dismissing him.

Despair descended upon Mike. He looked down at the useless petition clutched in his hand.

"Pssssst!" The sound came from across the room. Mike turned. A young man sitting in a chair in the corner beckoned to him.

"Don't let Bessie scare you," he said with a smile when the boy had joined him. "She's Mr. Drake's watch dog and, believe me, it isn't an easy job working for a human dynamo. She has to keep more people out than she lets in and they make a lot of trouble for her. It's a wonder she's as pleasant as she is." He pulled the corners of his mouth down as he said this and Mike had to grin. The young man held out his hand.

"I'm Jim Roberts of *The Crusader*. What's your trouble?"

Mike shook hands and sat down. He badly needed someone to tell him what to do now. He wished Mr. Moon was here but, since he wasn't, maybe this newspaper reporter could help.

Holding out the petition, he glanced to see if the secretary was watching. She was busy on the phone again, again saying no one could see Mr. Drake for the rest of the week. So he told Jim Roberts about the hut, about the City Manager's order, about the signatures on the petition. He didn't mention Mr. Moon. Sometimes it was hard for him to believe there was a Mr. Moon. Except for the handwriting on the petition, Mr. Moon might never have existed except in his imagination.

The reporter listened carefully, without interrupting, to the end. Then he began to ask questions, writing the answers down in a small notebook he carried. When had Mike decided to build the hut? Why? How long had it taken? What had the man from the Building Inspector's office said?

It was then Mike told him about going to see the Building Inspector.

"Charlie? You talked with Charlie?" the reporter asked.

"Yes," Mike said. "He's a real good guy, but I think I got him in trouble and I'm sorry."

When he told Jim Roberts about the City Manager getting mad at the Building Inspector, Jim nodded. "I know about that. I saw Charlie today and he told me he had sent Mr. Drake a written request for a public hearing. Once he got the City Manager's written notice about being suspended, he was so mad he blew up and swore he'd get his job back." He glanced at Mike. "Guess you know about that temper of his."

Mike nodded.

The reporter put his notes away and stood up. "Come on, young fellow," he said. "We've got things to do."

They went down the hall to a room with "PRESS" written on the door. Jim Roberts led Mike inside and introduced him to a man with a camera.

"We're going to get some pictures. This is the man who takes them for *The Crusader*."

The cameraman went to work. He took pictures of Mike alone, of Mike holding the petition, of the petition, and finally they went back down the hall and took one of Mike with his hand on the doorknob of the City Manager's office.

"Will you let me borrow the petition?" Jim asked.

"Sure," Mike answered. "It's no good if I can't get in to show it to Mr. Drake."

When they finished, Jim led Mike into the hall and pressed the elevator button. "Thanks," Mike said.

"Thanks to you for a good story," Jim Roberts replied. "It's a pleasure to write about something you believe in and I believe in your right to keep this hut. Now you just go home and don't worry. Sometimes a newspaper story helps."

Chapter

10

*A*t breakfast the next morning Mike's father took up his newspaper and let out a surprised roar. "What's this?" he asked. Mike leaned over to see and Mrs. McAllister got up from her end of the table to come and look.

There, on the front page, was Mike's picture. The headline above it read, "FUTURE ASTRONAUT DENIED RIGHT TO KEEP SPACE HUT." The story which followed continued on a back page where there were more pictures, of the hut, of the petition, showing clearly the curls and flourishes of Mr. Moon's flowing pen, and of Mike with his hand on the doorknob of the City Manager's office. Beneath this last picture were the words, "Mike McAllister turned away without a hearing."

His father gave him a long look, then spread the paper out on the table and read the whole story aloud. The reporter had written about the space age and boys who would be the spacemen of tomorrow. He told of his meeting with Mike and of learning about the petition. He told how the City Manager had started a campaign to clean up unsightly property in the city and had ordered Mike's hut torn down. He wrote that the Building Inspector had refused to carry out the order and a threat of suspension now hung over him.

Jim Roberts ended his story with: "This boy has been dreaming his dreams in an oak tree far above the ground. Now there are some people who don't hold with dreaming, who would say he should come back to earth and to reality. The question is, has anyone the right to keep this boy from reaching out toward that wonderful world above him? Should any man or any city be allowed to pull him back to earth for a selfish reason, watch out! If it can be done in this case, then beware of the future when other men will find other reasons to stop our astronauts from visiting those planets which have beckoned to man and stirred his imagination since the beginning of time!"

There was a silence when his father finished reading and Mike glanced at his mother. A faint smile was on her lips as she stood beside his father, and she nodded her head approvingly. "It's a beautiful article," she said softly.

Mike looked at his father. He had said the hut wasn't

important enough to fight for. Would he be angry now that it seemed someone else had decided it was?

Mr. McAllister turned his head toward the window which looked out upon the back yard. Then he stood up and laid the paper aside. "Let's have another look at this famous hut of yours, Mike."

With Beetlejuice draped about his shoulders, the boy followed his father outside. There was no sign of Mr. Moon as they approached the foot of the oak tree. Mike's father stood for a long time gazing at the space hut.

"Mind if I go up and have a look at it?" he finally asked. The clothes he wore on Saturdays when he worked on the recreation room in the basement were just right for climbing trees.

"No," Mike said, "I don't mind." Beetlejuice squeaked as Mr. McAllister started up the board steps, wanting to go too, but Mike stepped back, holding the small animal in his arms. "It's better if he goes alone," he whispered into his pet's short rounded ear.

Setting the skunk down, he sat on the ground at the foot of the tree. Beetlejuice sniffed the air, then ambled alongside the hedge, stopping now and then to dig an insect out of the ground with the long claws of his forefeet, to watch with bright eyes as a bird well out of reach taunted him with chatter and song.

It was here Charlie Monahan, the Building Inspector, found Mike after Mrs. McAllister directed him to the back yard. The big man came around the side of the house, his hat pushed to the back of his head. He waved a paper clutched in his right hand and called out a greeting so loudly that Beetlejuice, surprised, stamped his front feet in warning and turned his back in preparation for attack.

"It's okay," Mike said, seeing Mr. Monahan's eyes on the skunk. "He's harmless. He just wasn't expecting company."

Charlie Monahan looked up into the big oak and saw the space hut nestling among the branches decorated with new leaves. "So that's it," he said. "That's what's got everyone down at City Hall running in circles." He walked around the tree, peering up at every side of the structure. "Can't see anything unsightly about that."

"My dad's up there now looking it over. Want to go up?" Mike asked.

Before Mr. Monahan could answer, Mr. McAllister came out of the hut and started down. Once he was sure of his footing, he scampered down as nimbly as a squirrel. Mike had never seen him move so fast and freely before. When his father neared the ground he leaped, landing in front of Mike. He seemed ten years younger than when he had gone up into the tree.

"It's great up there, son," he announced enthusiastically. "Took me right back to my own boyhood. I'd forgotten what it's like to . . ." He noticed Charlie Monahan and looked at Mike questioningly.

"This is the Building Inspector, Dad. The one you read about in the newspaper a while ago."

After Mike found Beetlejuice and set him upon his

shoulder, the three of them went into the house. Once seated in the living room, Charlie Monahan handed the paper he'd been carrying to Mr. McAllister.

"I came over to see if you'd let Mike be a witness for me when I make my appeal. A meeting of the Personnel Board has been called for next week and I think maybe he could help me tell my side of the story. That paper is from the City Manager, giving the reasons he wants me removed from my job."

Mr. McAllister read the paper carefully. When he finished, his lips were twitching as though he found it hard to keep from laughing. "Looks like you were a one-man mutiny all right," he told the Inspector. "It says here you rebelled, revolted, and defied authority. Only thing he hasn't charged you with is high treason."

Charlie Monahan flushed. "Guess I did get a little stirred up. I have a quick temper, get my back up easy. I didn't mean any harm though. All I wanted was to see that this boy of yours got treated fairly, and that I was left alone to do my job properly, as I saw fit. I don't like anyone telling me how to run my office, especially not someone as new to the city as Mr. Drake is . . ." he made a face, "or as young. Anyway, what I need the boy as a witness for is to show I had a good reason to get mad. That hut isn't causing anyone any bother."

A half-hour later when the Building Inspector left, not only had Mike been given permission to testify, but Mr. McAllister had agreed to represent Charlie Monahan at the hearing.

Chapter

11

$\mathcal{M}$ike and his father were due at City Hall on Tuesday morning at ten o'clock. At breakfast Mrs. McAllister announced that she wished she could attend. "What they decide about Mr. Monahan is important," she declared, "because it will certainly affect what is to be done about Mike's hut. If I hadn't already promised to watch Bess Williams' baby for her this morning, I'd go along with the two of you."

Mike looked at her gratefully. It was good to find that his space hut was important not only to him but to others too.

"You'd better leave Beetlejuice in the basement," his mother went on. "With the baby around I'll feel better to have him closed up somewhere." She carried the dishes into the kitchen, calling back, "Oh, be sure to wear your sweater, Mike. It turned cooler last night."

Mike opened the back door. Beetlejuice, at his side, pressed his nose against the screen and squeaked his pleasure at the chill in the spring air. His thick hair bristled and his bushy tail waved approvingly.

"Can I leave him in the hut instead, Mom?" Mike asked. "This is his favorite kind of a day to be outdoors. And maybe he won't have a chance to go up much longer."

"All right. Take him up but don't stay. Your father'll be ready to leave soon."

As Mike pulled himself and his pet into the hut, he was pleased to see Mr. Moon there. Tucked snugly into a corner, wearing a windbreaker jacket against the change of weather, the little old man whittled away with his knife as usual, a half-stripped branch in his hand.

Mike hurriedly told him about the meeting.

"Seems everything's going to turn out all right," Mr. Moon said, nodding and laying aside his knife in order to stroke Beetlejuice who was climbing up his arm. "With the story in the newspaper letting everyone know what a fight you've put up for your hut, and now your father defending Mr. Monahan, it looks like things are going to turn out fine."

Mike wished he could feel as confident as that. His father believed that Mr. Drake was within his rights to ask for Mr. Monahan's suspension. "He shouldn't have talked back to his boss that way. No one can do a job if his helpers defy him."

"Why are you going to defend him then?" Mike had asked. "It sure sounds hopeless to me."

"Because there's more to it than that," Mr. Mc-Allister replied. "What I'll be defending will be your hut and Charlie Monahan's right to stand up for what he believes."

Mike heard his father call from the back door, "Hurry, son, I have to stop by the office on the way."

"I'm leaving Beetlejuice up here," Mike told the old man quickly. "He can't climb down, so he'll be safe."

He looked up once on the way to the ground and saw Mr. Moon sitting on the edge of the platform, watching the robins in the oak branches, his feet swinging idly in the air. Beetlejuice was draped lazily across his shoulders, watching too.

The public hearing was held at City Hall. When Mike and his father arrived, nearly every seat in the meeting room was taken. Mr. McAllister led the way to a large table at the front of the room where the five members of the City Personnel Board sat, each in front of a microphone. The member who was acting as chairman of the meeting placed his gavel on the notes he'd been making and glanced up as Mr. McAllister approached. Mike waited while his father exchanged greetings with the men, then followed him to a table at the right, with a microphone on it and chairs on one side. Back of these was a bench along the wall. At a nod from his father, he sat there. His father seated himself at the table.

Looking around the room, Mike saw that on the other side of the big table, there was another like the one at which his father sat. At this table, a young man was twiddling a pencil in his fingers and impatiently tapping his foot on the floor. In the space between, a stenotypist was limbering up his fingers on the keys of a machine on a stand before him, preparing to record the meeting.

Mike watched his father settle himself, lay his notes in front of him, and move the microphone closer. Then, becoming aware of sounds in the room, he listened to the rise and fall of the crowd's voices and to the loud ticking of a clock on a nearby wall. He turned to look at it just as its hands moved into the exact position of ten o'clock.

At that moment the Chairman of the Personnel Board leaned forward into his microphone and declared the meeting open. Charlie Monahan, puffing and panting, slid into a seat beside Mr. McAllister. Mike heard him say out of the corner of his mouth, "My wife claims I was even late to my own wedding."

Mr. McAllister was instructed to give the reasons for the hearing and after that to start calling witnesses for the Building Inspector. As his father recounted all that had taken place, Mike felt proud and thankful. It had taken his father a while to recognize how important

the space hut was but once he had, he was prepared to do all he could to save it.

The witnesses came forward, one after another. Each occupied a chair near Mr. McAllister's table and testified on Charlie Monahan's character, his loyalty, his training and experience, his dedication to his job. By the time the fifth witness was called, Mike noticed that the impatient young man across the way was fidgeting in his chair, and when the ninth prepared to take a seat, saw him lean forward and declare into the microphone, "Mr. Chairman, I must interrupt because I am a very busy man. In order to save time, I wish to state that I am in agreement as to Mr. Monahan's reputation and his past good record as a public servant. It is to the blemish which has recently appeared on that record that I feel we should now turn our attention . . . namely, his refusal to carry out orders from me, his superior. I appeal to the Board to take up the matter of Mr. Monahan's suspension at once so that we may hear its decision and get back to our duties as soon as possible."

Only then did Mike realize that the young man was Mr. Drake, the City Manager.

Mr. McAllister rose immediately to plead that he had not finished laying the groundwork for his case. There was a stirring in the crowd and the Chairman banged his table loudly with the gavel. When quiet had been restored, he announced a short recess, calling Mike's father, Mr. Drake, and Mr. Monahan to the long table for a conference.

Waiting for things to start up again, Mike passed the time by looking over the crowd. The architect who had signed the petition raised his clasped hands in a gesture of encouragement when the boy's eyes found him. Farther along the rows, he came across Jim Roberts who waved a hand in greeting, and *The Crusader*'s photographer who nodded his head. To his great amazement, in one of the seats at the end of a nearby row, he saw Mr. Moon. The old man had evidently been watching him. Now, having caught Mike's attention, he half-way unzipped his jacket and out of the opening popped a small black head. Two curious bright eyes surveyed the surroundings. Mr. Moon had brought Beetlejuice to the hearing!

Chapter
12

$\mathcal{A}$t eleven twenty-two by the clock on the wall, Mike was called to take the witness chair.

"Now, Michael," Mr. McAllister said formally, "tell us about your space hut. Tell us what it means to you and how you feel about Mr. Drake's ordering it destroyed."

Mike saw Mr. Drake wince at the word "destroy," frown, lean forward as if to protest, then change his mind and sit back.

At first the boy spoke hesitantly, conscious of the eyes upon him, of many ears listening. But when he began to describe how he felt sitting up in the top of the oak tree, the words rushed out so fast that his father had to lay a hand on his arm to slow him down.

"Did you try explaining all this to anyone, Michael?"

The boy nodded. "To Mr. Monahan. He understood. He had a tree hut when he was young and he knew just how I felt about mine."

"To anyone else?" his father asked.

Mike glanced at the City Manager. "I tried to take the petition to Mr. Drake and explain to him too but I couldn't get in." Remembering how Jim Roberts had called Bessie, the secretary, a watch dog for the official, he added, "You're supposed to have an appointment, but I don't think anyone ever gets one. He's too busy. It's like . . . like . . ."—a phrase Mr. Moon had used once came back to him—"if he took his finger off the button, the world might stop turning."

The audience laughed. Since the hearing began, it had seen the City Manager twiddling his pencil, tapping his foot, fidgeting in his chair. To them it was plain that Mr. Drake was a young man with no time to spare, dedicated to keeping his finger on that button.

The City Manager flushed. Taking up his microphone, he demanded in an annoyed voice, "Mr. Chairman, just who is on trial here today? First I am made to seem like some kind of ogre who goes around destroying children's playthings. Now I am forced to defend myself against . . ." He stopped, drowned out by the crowd.

Now I've done it, Mike thought. I've made him mad. The Chairman banged his gavel on the desk and the audience slowly quieted down. "Let's move along," he said. "I suggest we now . . ."

Another commotion erupted. It started as gasps from women; then men cleared their throats, and in a few seconds people began rising to their feet. Mike, turning to see what was causing the disturbance, got a jolting shock. There, as carefree as if he were strolling along the hedge in the back yard looking for insects, was Beetle-juice, sauntering across the room.

Horrified, Mike looked for Mr. Moon who should have been right behind the runaway skunk, but there was no sign of the little old man anywhere.

Leaping up, the boy ran to pick up his pet. He held him close and said loudly so that the whole room could hear, "It's all right. He's harmless. He's tame."

Slowly the crowd settled down again, looking sheepish, ashamed to have taken alarm over such a small black creature, now curled in the crook of the boy's arm.

Instead of going back to the seat near his father, Mike walked over and stood in front of Mr. Drake. "Honestly," he said, "I wasn't trying to be funny a minute ago. If I said anything wrong, I'm sorry. I just thought I should have had a chance to see you that day in the office, to tell my side of the story." He shrugged and the skunk held on tight, digging his claws into the cloth of Mike's sleeve.

"It was my fault, I guess, that you and Mr. Monahan got mad and yelled at each other. It wouldn't have happened if it hadn't been for my space hut."

To Mike's surprise, the City Manager didn't seem to

be listening to a thing he was saying. No longer was Mr. Drake the jumpy young man of a few minutes ago. Instead, he was leaning forward, his hands clasped quietly before him, his eyes misty as they dwelt on Beetlejuice.

There was a wistful smile on his face as he said, "I had a skunk just like yours when I was about your age. Used to carry him around the same way too. I found him abandoned in the Arizona desert when he was a baby. Fed him on eggs and milk and insects. I guess all I did that whole summer vacation was catch bugs for him."

A shadow passed over the young man's face. "I brought him home with me in the fall, but one day he got loose and a neighbor thought he was wild and shot him. The man didn't give me a chance to explain."

He looked up at Mike suddenly. "What does yours eat?"

"Mostly bugs. An egg once in a while, and sometimes he catches mice." Mike placed the skunk on the table in front of Mr. Drake. Beetlejuice sniffed curiously at the microphone, examining it with his paws. His sudden squeaks into it sounded loudly throughout the room and sent the watching people into shouts of laughter. Startled, Beetlejuice sought the nearest refuge, the shoulder of the City Manager.

The young man reached up and gently stroked the animal. "I hadn't thought about that summer for a long time," he said in a surprised voice. "I'd forgotten what it's like to be eleven or twelve years old." He looked hard at Mike, then grinned. "Do you get mad easy?"

"I don't know," Mike said. "Sometimes." Then he grinned back at Mr. Drake. "I sure got mad when I heard somebody wanted to tear down my space hut."

For several moments there was silence. Then the City Manager stood up, Beetlejuice still on his shoulder. As he came around the table, he reached up, took the skunk and handed it to Mike.

"You're right. You did deserve a chance to tell your side of the story. I didn't give you that, did I? I didn't give it to someone else either."

He crossed the room to where Charlie Monahan was sitting. "I take it all back," he said, loud enough for everyone to hear. "I'm canceling the order to tear down the tree hut. I apologize, Mr. Monahan, for what I said to you and about you. You do a good job and I hope you'll be with the city for a long time."

The crowd cheered as the City Manager and the Building Inspector shook hands. Photographers took pictures, there was a lot of confusion, and everyone talked at once.

Mike stood thinking of Mr. Moon and wondering why, all of a sudden, he was absolutely sure the old man was gone for good. Ever since he had looked around the room and not found him, the boy had known.

He sighed, guessing the mystery of the little old man would never be solved. But he knew that whenever he sat up in his space hut, whenever he saw a robin in the branches of the oak tree, whenever he looked up at the stars in the evening and dreamed of exploring them someday, he would think of Mr. Moon. Wherever Mr. Moon was, Mike knew he would be helping someone who needed him.

Beetlejuice dug his claws into Mike's arm and squeaked contentedly in his ear. "Well," he seemed to be saying, "didn't I tell you to call on me whenever the going got rough?"